# Happy Christmas, Rita!

# Happy Christmas, Rita!

## Hilda Offen

Happy Cat Books

*For Lucy and Sally Gill*

**HAPPY CAT BOOKS**

Published by Happy Cat Books Ltd.
Bradfield, Essex CO11 2UT, UK

This edition first published 2001
3 5 7 9 10 8 6 4 2

A CIP catalogue record for this book is available from the British Library

ISBN 1 903285 26 7

Printed in Hong Kong by Wing King Tong Co. Ltd.

It was the day before Christmas.

"It's snowing!" said Rita.

"Hurray!" cried Julie. "I'll go skating!"

"And we can take the sledge out!" said Jim and Eddie.

"You'll all have to wait until the snow stops!" said Mrs Potter.

5

In the afternoon the sun came out and the Potter children ran to put on their outdoor clothes.

"Where's my coat?" asked Rita. "And my wellingtons? I left them in a bag by the door."

"A yellow plastic bag?" asked Eddie.
"Oops! Sorry, Rita! I thought they were
jumble. I gave them to the lady from the
Dogs' Home."

"You'll have to stay in, Rita!" called Mrs
Potter. "You can't go out without your
warm clothes."

Rita watched as the children raced away.
She felt really sad. Then she had an idea.

"My Rescuer's outfit!" she said.

She raced upstairs and took the box from
under her bed.

She put on her tights, her tunic and her
cloak. She put on her yellow gloves and her
belt. And last of all she put on her boots
with wings on the heels. Rita Potter had
disappeared! In her place stood – Rita the
Rescuer!

"Here we go!" cried Rita and she zoomed
out of the window. She felt as warm as
toast!

As Rita flew up the street she
spotted little Robbie Russell.
He was looking at a snowflake
through his magnifying glass.

"Look out, Robbie!" shouted
the people round about.

A giant icicle had fallen from
the roof above him!

"He's had it!" gasped
the crowd.

"Not while I'm here!" cried Rita, and she puffed as hard as she could. Her hot breath melted the icicle and turned it into a shower of rain. Little Robbie was soaked.

"Never mind!" said Rita, and she huffed and puffed him dry again.

Suddenly a scream rang out.

"Got to go!" cried Rita.

"I recognise that voice."

Jim and Eddie's sledge had taken a
wrong turn. It was heading for the quarry!
"Help!" screamed Jim and Eddie.

Rita cut through the cold air like a knife. She pulled the sledge to a halt on the edge of a sheer drop.

"It's the Rescuer again!" gasped Eddie.

Rita dragged them back up the hill and pushed them down the safe slope.

"Be more careful in future!" she called.

At the bottom of the hill Mrs Simpkins was digging like mad.

"I've lost my dog, Tiger!" she cried. "I think he's buried somewhere in this snow-drift."

"I'll find him for you," said Rita. "I have X-ray eyes."

She took the shovel from Mrs Simpkins
and snow flew everywhere as she dug
deeper and deeper into the drift. In no time
at all she had lifted Tiger out of the snow.

"Thank you, thank you!" cried Mrs
Simpkins; but Rita couldn't stay to chat.
She had heard more screams and a loud
cracking sound!

Julie and her best friend Tania were
skating on the pond. Oh no! The ice was
beginning to crack.

"They'll be drowned!" cried the people
on the bank.

"No they won't!" said Rita. She grabbed
Julie and Tania just as the ice gave way
beneath them. Then she flew them back to
the edge of the pond.

"Thanks, Rescuer!" said Julie. "Can we
have your autograph?"

But Rita wasn't listening. A low rumbling
filled the air. It got louder and louder and
louder.

A giant snowball was rolling towards the town. It rumbled on, getting bigger and bigger all the time.

"Help!" cried the people. "The town will be destroyed!"

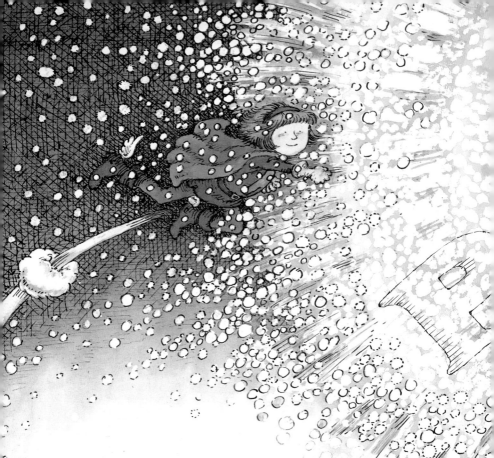

Rita moved with the speed of light.

Pow! She hit the snowball as hard as she could. It burst into a million trillion pieces and fell like snow on to the roof-tops beneath.

"Hurray!" cheered the crowd. "The Rescuer's saved our town!"

No one could thank Rita enough. They
built a huge snow Rescuer in the Market
Place and Rita helped them with the
difficult bits.

"It will stay there until the snow melts," said the mayor, "to remind us of the day you saved us, Rescuer!"

"I'm glad I could help!" said Rita.

It was beginning to get dark, so Rita started off for home. On the way she passed Basher Briggs, who was snowballing some toddlers.

"Let's see how *you* like it!" said Rita, and she threw a hundred snowballs at Basher, all within the space of a second.

"Stop!" yelled Basher. "I'll never do it again – I promise!"

"Well – that was a good day's work!"
thought Rita as she sped through the starry
sky. "Hallo! What's that?"

Two boots were sticking out of a chimney pot. Some reindeer stamped their hooves nearby.

Rita swooped down. She grasped the boots and pulled as hard as she could. "One – two – three – heave!" she cried.

There was a Pop! and a shower of soot – and out shot Father Christmas!

"I must have had one mince-pie too many!" he said. "I'm sure I got down that chimney last year. Thank you, Rescuer!"

"It was a pleasure!" said Rita. "Happy Christmas, Father Christmas!"

"The same to you!" he said.

Rita flew back home and changed into her ordinary clothes. Then she went downstairs.

Eddie, Julie and Jim were decorating the Christmas tree.

"What a shame you had to stay indoors, Rita!" said Jim. "You missed the Rescuer again!"

"She stopped our sledge from falling into the quarry!" said Eddie.

"She grabbed me and Tania just as we were about to go through the ice!" said Julie.

"She saved the town from being flattened by a giant snowball!" cried Jim.

"Well, I never!" said Rita.

On Christmas morning Rita woke early.
At the end of her bed was a gigantic
stocking – the biggest one she had ever
seen!

It was bursting with toys and books and
sweets. There was even a new coat and a
pair of boots.

"Happy Christmas, everyone!" cried
Rita.